You Arrived in the Season of Perennial Summer

You Arrived in the Season of Perennial Summer

New collection of poems by Lee Young-ju
Translated by Jae Kim

5ǫǫ

K

POET

아시아

Contents

YOU ARRIVED
IN THE SEASON
OF PERENNIAL
SUMMER

POET

Plain Notebook

You fell into the depths from a tall cliff and arrived here, in the back of a drawer. A blank notebook, a spirit whispers.

Our fear leads us to speak in a certain way.

In your tracksuit
you dine alone in silence at the dinner table.

Who would have thought this was the bottom of the cliff.

Who would have thought you'd arrive here, having fallen from here.

The Taste of Glaciers

The multifaceted nature of hell. I want to get out. Like grief, I'm stuck between the ice. But you're able to hold everything in your gaze, even death, like the inside of a glass globe crafted to contain ashes. People used to talk, walking all over me. Passing by, they would turn back toward the night, into which a large piece of ice would have dropped. Who would have thought they could see so much in such darkness, I must go home before dark! I ran. I was good at running. I sprinted and was trapped in the ice. No one could cure my night blindness. In the dark, one can hear the sound of heavy feet and fast feet bumping into each other. An old man, who has realized he can't draw the map of the whole world and has returned after many centuries, is breaking up the ice. Why won't you melt even though spring has come? The old man looks at me and shakes his head. One can be lost anywhere on earth. I'm stuck in grief. It tastes like a glacier.

The Daily Life of a Café Owner

The storytellers of Damascus have gathered in this caf   for many centuries. I can't close shop.

The storytellers come together under the light and ask about each other's love lives. They ask about the most awful subject in the world. One of them sinks into his chair and says that a life form grows delicately from being treaded on gently

talks about a gloomy heart while no one listens. He's come face to face with the dark life form that grows little by little beside his chair. How can they stay gathered around the table for such a long time with their heads put together? Their glued-together heads stink of an addicting dream.

When you unfold the dream, a black stain spreads.

Time will come to an end today, they say. What a ridiculous affair. One of them, sinking into his chair, turns darker. The leechlike day is attached to his back. You're not supposed to eat sugar, never

burnt sugar. They wash their sticky bowls. The dishwashing repeats daily. It can't stop.

They say when you become too sweet, you might suffer consequences

but the storytellers of Damascus are sucking on their lips. Delicious. Joyful.

I'm sitting here today. I've journeyed across the first page of a story that might just melt away. I've journeyed away from my daily life. This story begins from the ruins.

Time's drinking blood, latched onto someone's back.

A Closed Butchery

In an expansive window

My cheeks are ripening in the cold

What is the square footage of my left cheek

My maternal grandmother appeared in front of me
after she died

I didn't understand when she told me she was
growing black hair

The hand that extends from inside touches the
flesh of my hand

Sometimes time grows younger after death

At dawn the display window melts and the black hair grows long

In front of the enormous window, Grandmother is staring at the crimson glow

She puts a piece of meat in her mouth and chews carefully for a long time

One's beautiful dwelling place, there are so many mysteries in the meat of a person

Mysteries like those fingernails and toenails that grow even after one dies

Dormitory

A hundred years ago, I was a young weaver. I ran out of the factory after two days, wrapped in yarn, a powerless ball of yarn. I sewed the air randomly and turned into a useless piece of cloth. I was a deprived person, drifting through the back alleys like a ghost. Amid songs of revolution outside the window, I was like the teeth of the dogs who crawled toward the blankets swept away by soldiers. Eating clouds that had fallen in the mud . . . *She stops singing by herself and looks in the mirror. A master of metamorphosis, she's disoriented, and she looks inward to orient herself, to know where she is in time. Sis. Sis, you're barely twenty-three years old, I say, cleaning the foggy mirror.* Often a light came on in my head. Whenever I coughed, washing rags in steel buckets, the light flickered on and off, and each time the factory closed down, my friends and I, wearing pale faces, were chased out onto the streets. But we wrapped gauze around our legs and shared cold rice. *Sis. Sis, you've never even read a book. Your sense of time is completely messed up, I say, turning out the light in the room. With the light out, birds could be seen tumbling toward the ground outside the window.* While we fell, we saw our friends hanging onto spires and fluttering like white towels. Home is an avalanche of grief, they say. In this mud are the empty hours that a hundred years couldn't fill. There was me, the young me who worked the sewing machine, left alone in the burning factory.

There were so many of me. *Sis. Sis, put down the pillow you're hugging, it has blood on it. Your song is too long and too frightening. I pull the blanket over her shoulders. I open a thick dictionary in the dark. The tumbling birds had nowhere to land.*

Dyer

Some people make colors to put food on the table. The sun has always ensured that it is reborn. A man sits in front of a stone. A man who cannot part with the stone because the light of Shiva is blue. A man who is dyed blue from his fingernails to the tips of his toenails. *I feel nauseous.* Father keeps sticking his head in the sewer. A god once brought the worst poison in the world with him on a journey. The blade of the shovel enters the stone but suddenly bends. Why did the god disappear with the poison? And why did he become blue? A dyer's children jump up and down irregularly like a heart on drugs. Under the reborn sun the children dye muslin. Father vomits after work. Our house is blue all over.

Like veins. It becomes quiet as the moonlight seeps in through the window. A man who disappeared into the veins of light. Why would anyone bring poison on his journey? A single drop of which could destroy humanity. That the god drank poison and all that happened was his neck turned blue is far too romantic. Humans, on the other hand, cannot seem to die. After making colors Father gets hungry and hardens into a blue lump. Is it really poison that Shiva brought on his journey? They say color doesn't exist to the man who can't see what's in front of him. Do you think that Father could shovel his way through this stone to attain blindness? The color of the stone a madman is digging through.

What do you think the blind god has left behind? The blade of the shovel sometimes lands on my feet. Father falls asleep next to the stone. What remains in the world is a blue addiction. A man who sticks his head in the stone and cannot leave. What is a god? Every day, the children who survive him break off twigs to dig under their fingernails dyed blue by the light. Until red blood pours out. They can finally feel the blood circulating through their bodies.

History

Wandering through dreams, he heard stories about a man who sold death. It seems those who want to feel rather than think don't know what to do with the tragedy of their lives and end up selling their deaths. The old man asleep in the alley, who had lived for far too long as an old man—ever since he was a boy—had nothing left to sell, now that he'd traversed a world. Not grief, not laughter, nothing but his body, which no one wanted to buy. No one could see his old and blackening body. Snuggling up to the wall, he wrapped his body in a blanket and tried opening his tangerine box, but only rotten tangerines rolled around inside. Things are always being collected, so why does the blanket remain in place? The bureau for environmental beautification collected the same blanket each night and ate his tangerines. It was the kind of night that made you drop your head and look at your heart. It was the kind of night in which black hair rained down from the sky. Time is said to be the name of the world in India. Oh, the one who feels time despite having received no revelations, the old man tried calling to himself. Oh, the one who feels the spirit of the blanket. The old man tried feeling himself. It is said that those who bought grief and those who bought laughter, they all sank in the water and died beautiful deaths. Oh, the one with the long black hair that falls to the ground, who remains alone and hands out all those deaths, said the old man. My time doesn't end, so I have plenty of hair. Hair that's never been cut, draped over the wall. The dark spirit stared at his heart from which white cotton flowed the way it flows from an unfinished blanket. Flesh being torn to pieces . . . It was a winter's night no one would buy. Wandering through dreams, he heard stories about a man carrying piles of death he could not sell.

Singer-Songwriter

I only listen to songs by dead singers. If we're talking about songs, songs of the dead taste best. You're alive, so your voice is dull. I stood in the corner and drank. As if I were about to vomit. Could I catch death, like an infection? Dead people sing well. Such fragrant songs. I left my head in the club. I have to go look for it. A place overflowing with dead singers' songs. The upside-down head of a hare in the butchery. I've walked there. You're alive, so you don't sing very well. Don't make the living sing. I ran like a hare. Let's only listen to dead singers' songs. Let's listen once. Let's listen again. Let's stand in the corner and listen. I open my sheet music. I left my head in the club, so the song sags and drips. Evening approaches. Like a red song, evening approaches. If we're talking about songs, then my songs, the ones on display, taste best. You're alive, so go ahead and crumple those pages of sheet music. Crumple your day-to-day living. I bring out a dead poet's notebook. The songs are gone, only the dead poet has stayed. Where did this woman disappear to? After drinking, I got lost and took a walk in your heart, which was filled with parasites. I sniffed around. Wanting to listen to infected songs. I left my head on an island I've never been to. Where did the dead poet go? Where did the song go? Drooling, I grip the mic tight in my hands.

Insomnia

When I turn on the light and lie face down, inside me, that light won't go out. I've read and read your letter, I've read it so much I've lost my memory.

Our bodies' flaws make us think of ourselves as being different from other animals. I sniff around. What's this smell? When I hold your hand, I feel a deep night. If there's an animal called night—did it leave tears on your palm?

That which you keep licking. That which spreads in the damp.

Go to sleep. Go to sleep.

You become a person by going to sleep.

On the inside of the window, you're crawling. Since I couldn't show you everything as-is, I wore the same clothes as you. Tonight, I need tens of thousands of souls because I want to become a different animal.

I wonder what you think you are. Did you leave fire in my hand? I peeled off one small soul at a time and threw them in the fire

hating people, loving people. The fire grew larger and larger, burning all my memories. What does this hollowed-out body think I am? In the depths of my room, I immediately ran into a brick wall. It recognized me.

You Come Walking Out of
My Dream

It's snowing. We're trapped in time. Let's begin our winter trip from the house. We drift alone on one road, alongside pain on another road. We're on a trip, aren't we? I was so relaxed I couldn't stand up. You're shivering. Like a hurt donkey. A trip in which we're home, bracing our heads. Will the pain be kind here? At dawn, you come walking out of my dream and beckon other people. *If we can get out of here, there's a beautiful suicide tree. Let us drift together. Until our long ears become dark as the night.* I shouldn't be writing dark sentences until morning. Your feet lie crushed in the light. When your eyes touch the window, inexplicable tears well up and make them slick. You're eating dark seaweed on your birthday. Let's see what's next on the menu . . .

Transience and Eternity

You're looking at me Leaning on the telephone pole
  I flow through the power lines

You hold fire in your hand Insisting you have experience living as an undead tree in a desert Here or there, I'm thirsty all the same, you say, and pour a little fire in your mouth You're thirsty because of all that is deepening

You said you cried yourself dry, with your roots in red soil, remembering eternity Crumbling into pieces will only take a moment Whenever I cry, ashes fall This is only a dream, all you did was walk into your dream like a flame, arms around the telephone pole

  You're as scary as a burnt tree, starved for thousands of years
  but water is all that flows through my soul, how could that be

  I don't have any experience living or dying, I go with the flow Without a beginning, without an end, fearlessly

  My headache trickles like a stream, and I've been thrown into the wetlands The stream keeps on

flowing even though I want to clench my two fists
Look at me The gathered sounds of sobbing smell
rotten

You arrived in the season of perennial summer
You arrived with your face burnt

We stand face to face in a clearing
groping for each other's demolished selves

While I flow away
you remain a thirsty tree
a tree that came walking out of my dream burning

You and I, who are so close we are sometimes confused for one another
confused for one another

You and I, who long to color and destroy each other
other

The burnt spot is wet

A chair has been placed over the spot

Roadside Tree

The tree had nowhere to go. Because from within, it couldn't completely fill its body with tears. In the heat wave, a black dog peed on the roots. I was running to a place, but I didn't know where I was going. A boy fell from the balcony of an apartment. Had he become part of yet another family? Dead people whose tears haven't dried are hanging from the tree. Oblivious to the fact that there is something somewhere that would make me cry, I became, at some point, a red summer. A leaf grew thick.

House of Tears
—in remembrance of the Jeju uprising

Water leaks from crushed knees. The boy stays in the basement for a long time, his head buried between his knees. Out of nowhere, the bone bits fell out and rolled around in the dirt. Why aren't we dead yet? they whisper, scattering. We were told long ago that we were dead. Why are we able to go on living? The boy is wrapped in hair that glows golden. Squirming like a caterpillar. Even in hell, you're supposed to be able to last until your soul meets its demise as long as there's water. The boy's been drinking his tears for many decades. Thirsty, he's replaying sad scenes in his mind. Remembering his brother's burning head. The fire was started by an acquaintance. Didn't know anything. Did it knowingly. There's a moment in which one can survive death. Because of that moment, some are not able to die. Such fate exists. In the house of fire, the boy let all the water in his body drain. Put out the fire. The fire ought to be put out. In the deepest basement, the bones of the boy flow through the veins of the water.

Work Team Leader

Humanity, begone! I mutter in the sewer as people aboveground pass by in droves. Is it possible? Is extinction possible? I go deeper, lie facedown, and start to suspect it's not. In a place even deeper, an electrician is at work. Oops, he says, having dropped his flashlight, and moves further into the depths. I lower myself into the suspicious depths with open eyes. He's in here, somewhere in this sewer. He's army-crawling, searching for the flashlight. He stops and searches inside himself. If the flashlight is inside him, where is this flickering light coming from? He manages the project forever. Since he's here in this sewer, where shapeless shapes are plenty, extinction is unlikely. I stand at the end of an invisible procession, unsure which way to go. There will be light if and only if I connect this power line to that power line! he shouts inward. No one can hear him. He cultivated his insides in Saudi Arabia. He realized, ingesting the salt from the Dead Sea, that he might not have to sink to the bottom. He figured out he might not have to die on a burning sheet of rusty steel. I didn't have a good feel for the charges that flowed through the power lines, so I sat down in a corner and peeked inside him. Sometimes he stroked my hair. If I go in deep, will I reach the end of the procession? Is someone there trying to bring about extinction? Above the sewer, humans are disappearing in droves. He stands in the dark and miserable spot. He who looks for the flashlight

in order to bring this power line and that power line

together. I grow ill, anxious to turn off the light. The

light doesn't go out no matter how deep we go.

The Neighborhood of Daebang

I used to fall asleep underneath the stairs. A list for the evening. It might be that we're clutching each other's hearts in a place we can't see. Why do you look away? Been a while since we forgot each other's faces. The simmering miso soup. I stared at the smudge on the earthenware after scooping everything into the soup. Mother. Burnt ashes. Sweet smoke was beginning to leak out into the corridor. Mother washed her hair on the anniversary of the day I disappeared. She dipped her hair into her tears in the basin. The list is soaked with smells. A glance at the window between sleep and life. The punishment that is the evening, I wrote on the wall, and thought about my ailment. Wearing my parka inside out, I wondered how I should drop and roll. Mother, you might dissolve into the wind like ashes, seeing how beautiful I am. My ailment flowed toward a place I was trying to get to, the road beyond the stairs, beyond the evening, where clenched teeth melted away. My ailment is more like an ailment because it's nothing. A dim playground. I preferred ruin of the kind in which shards of glass pierced the bottom of my feet. The stairs were ailing because mysterious carcasses have stiffened and formed a secret pattern. Why was the evening invented? The skeleton in the cupboard, as in the European saying, was moving on to another ailment. Tears falling like the tears from your wet hair. Mother, it was nice there.

Puberty

Waking up from a dream is the grandest nightmare, isn't it? When crossing over from darkness to light.

Mother, please don't wake me at times like this.

But she shakes me all the more. Could it be you're dying? You'll disappear before me? Time is evil and welcoming. Come back to this moment. Grow up again, and grow old again.

Crossing over from darkness to light. I must nurse my pain inside a greater light. You can't leave me in this moment.

A child wordlessly kneads mud with two hands.

Eats mud, buries her face in mud, and burrows deeper, deeper toward the bottom. No matter how far she falls, she's in the blood-soaked mud. Burrow into that mud, and there's more dirt.

Mother cries, squeezing the back of the child's head.

Summer Vacation

On the first night of the vacation stories abound. That moment when I meet eyes with my self, who, next to my sleeping self, is laughing with her mouth torn open. Something good must have happened, since I'm laughing. Is this what it means to tell ghost stories in the summer? Falling asleep again, I run my fingers over my torn lips. Did I laugh too much? I run my fingers over the mime's lips. To be with the self, looking at the self. To be able to see the faceless self. We eat omelets and share joyful stories. This cypress table is supposed to absorb moisture very well, so it's the perfect place for sharing lies. We sweat our bile. Insects can't climb onto the cypress table. Why do you insist on touching only the dark things? When you watched me feel my chest, around my heart, I laughed. According to Pascal, the greatest tragedy is the fact that the soul which looks at the self exists together with the self. You laughed, too. If I can fall asleep, I should be able to throw myself away. You came here to take a walk. You went deep into the mountains. The reason time is falling apart is because we're burning. It's a night of eating pork ribs and writing kind words of condolence. The lip of the forest is supposed to open when it's time to erase the self. To sweat our bile, we lower our heads. On the plate is a pile of cooled bones. There are many caterpillars around me, squirming. I plan to sit down and read this letter of condolence alone.

Metropolis

I receive a bouquet of flowers It's okay It's not like the flowers a person gifts You tell me it's okay You who are neither man nor woman hand me a heavy load that is like a bouquet of flowers I didn't buy You cry the rowdy cry of bugs in a flower Even though a young child told me to buy them Now that I think about it you don't have an age You say not having an age is not so bad *Puh puh puh,* the hard insects spit it out Too much pours out, since they don't have teeth Drooling, you take off Dragging me, my ankleless self who wandered too much day after day in a previous life When we fall asleep at the corner of a building, a wind more terrifying, much longer and thicker, than the wind elsewhere blows

It's okay The blue flesh the wind has eaten is the flesh I threw away in a previous life Come to think of it, in all my previous lives, I only ever took walks in buildings Stuck in the crevices of the old walls, like my flesh, are your cries, those you've given me To peel each one off the walls, I walked in buildings I felt okay as long as I was eating It was delicious Anxious to leave this donut of time, I look to you, oil dripping down my chin It's okay You don't look like a cleaning lady if you hold flowers It's okay, you say, and hand me a flower. The long hair, unraveled, grows, like a broom, longer and longer So much has been lost, and yet, you pull

my luggagelike self to you and push me into you
You offer flowers It's fine We can wither together
You remain in place after the underground train has
departed

I'll cut you a flowering tree

I take the sharpest blue axe and go marching inside
you

Shrubland

Let's be healthy. We must fall into a deep sleep. Though I've never been able to sleep. On his bed in the hospital, my uncle gathers puzzle pieces in his sleep. Who dropped them? I bury my face in the pillow and open my eyes. I can't see anything. I think I've seen this kind of intimacy in the hellscape I once drew.

My uncle strokes my hair as I lie face down. *Sleep is very important.*

They say there are many dead youths in the forest. In order to be reborn, they hung from trees for seven days and seven nights. They say you can learn a word, a word that grips you as would the roots of trees. My uncle opens his notebook and writes, *shrubland.*

These tales are in books, tales of youths being reborn, tales of them returning . . . Since a person is also part of nature, call me a tree when I die. I can't read my uncle's writing.

This intimate hellscape is an old tale. One must carry an empty notebook to the forest.

House of Tears

Only good people come to graves. As the medieval saying goes, you're as old as your dying self the moment you are born. He throws the shovel and sits down.

Those who come to graves are all good people. Humans are familiar with tears from the moment they're born. If we don't cry, he says, we die. He slaps his butt in an exaggerated fashion and places a cigarette between his lips.

This grave is so bogged down with water even good people will rot. Why do we put so much effort into maintaining our form when we're dead? Pay me extra, he says. Raising the corner of his mouth, he smiles.

He's my family. A good person. The gravedigging, a sacred act, isn't for me to write down. When I open the casket, bugs engorged with tears are squirming inside.

1.

Jeju, raining.

I was by myself.

I was disoriented and afraid because of it,

and because I felt awkward about life, I cried a

little at the airport.

I was dreaming of a cozy downfall.

But the beautiful and kind people around me always

manage to keep misfortune at bay.

2.

They may only be a part of the process of tipping

over from life to death, but there are moments of

brilliance.

When I hold hands with you in the cold wind.

And that sugary muffin.

3.

A transparent poem no one has written. The downfall begins to shine beautifully . . .

4.

I was walking down the street of Jeongdong for work, and I was reminded of the time in my life when I would go to the city art museum with Hyeongjin and have coffee at Jeongwangsu Coffee. We were a little excited that day, weren't we? Let's not cry, dear friend. Not everything in life will be difficult.

5.

Times like this are no good. They're too distant from the root cause. I think I was a weaver in a factory a hundred years ago. Maybe a handweaver for hire a thousand years ago. I'm now weaving things that aren't easily woven. Language? What language? I fail each time. When I fail, I can feel a faint presence of the roots . . . .

6.

Even if my heart doesn't reach others' . . . it's all right. Much love, then, to myself for trying.

I Wore Glasses

This world is full of misery. Every day, I think of exile.

I was nineteen when I wrote this in a journal entry. How full of herself was she?

For a person to develop a sense of self, they need an object to set themselves equal to. The object doesn't have to be a person. Whether it be a person or a rock, we're thrown into the uncertain world of violence. That person and that rock and I, we all come from different backgrounds. We can't help but be different. We were born—and we will die— in different places. And the rock won't even die. Of course the order of our deaths is subject to change.

Equating means we want all four corners of the drawer to fit perfectly. Such greedy nonsense. Meanwhile we burn in this unstable hell and turn to ashes. Who is this person breathing on the ashes to scatter them? Who is this person saying, Idiots. Take a look at your greed!

I've worn glasses for a long time now. I think I was nine or ten when I began wearing them. I was sitting under a warm sun, and I suddenly felt one of my eyes turn off like a light bulb. Darkness pierced through the light and entered my eye. I rubbed my eyes, but it was no use. I felt a heavy stone was weighing down on my eyeball. Afterwards, I rubbed the eye that showed darkness every chance I got. Occasionally, I told my mom. Mom, I think a worm lives in my eye.

One day, in a lot behind my apartment, I was focusing on assembling a toy and couldn't hear anything. I was run over by a bicycle. Because of the worm in my eye, I had a habit of turning my head to one side, and the wheel of the bicycle that an older boy in the neighborhood was riding came straight into my eye. A great world of darkness enveloped my whole body.

For a while I went through therapy to mend the jagged pieces of flesh around my eye. Throughout the therapy, I had to wipe away the blood that dripped from my eye and change the dressing every day.

One day, I was on my way to the hospital as usual, holding my mom's hand. Suddenly a viscous liquid dripped into my mouth. A boy walking toward us with a man pointed a finger at me. He swallowed his spit and spoke either to me or to the man beside him.

"Hey, look, blood."

When she heard this, my mom frantically

produced a handkerchief and applied pressure on the wound that had reopened. I kept bleeding. The white handkerchief quickly turned red. I watched the boy's finger as it multiplied and spread outward. I tried to look with my remaining eye. The boy's finger kept getting smushed in my vision. Hey, look, blood. Look, blood. Blood. Blood.

I wonder why I didn't cry out loud. I quietly shed tears. Fear and uncertainty got jumbled up together and I didn't want to scream. I only shed those tears, which were hotter than the blood. My mom lifted me into her arms and began running to the hospital. I could feel her desperate breathing and her racing heartbeat. I could also see that strange sentence being written in the air: Hey, look, blood.

After the wounds around my eye healed, I started wearing glasses all the time. I took an eye exam, and we learned that the eye would never recover. I felt at ease when I put on my glasses. I learned that no matter how anxious you feel, that anxiety will ease at some point. Even with glasses, my vision was terrible, I was nearly blind, and I showed no signs of improvement year after year. Things were stripped of their borders, blended into one another, and approached me as one big lump. Thankfully my remaining eye allowed me to distinguish them, and I was satisfied. It's a blessing to be able to see things the way other people see them. Even if it's with one eye.

A small scar remains. A cheap-looking deep scar. And I became alone. I could no longer be the same as any object I beheld. Since I couldn't see accurately, I saw vaguely, and I didn't know how to set things equal anymore. My mom and dad didn't wear glasses, and the god I'd learned about didn't have a bad eye. Though this god didn't have a form of his own, his son had a good-looking

Mediterranean man's face.

My body turned into an eye. In order to concentrate on looking at something, my whole body tensed up. I also turned my head to the side to have my good eye do the looking. I felt my face was being gathered to one side. My arms and legs were tense, and my heart rate often went through the roof. Sometimes I lowered my head and closed my eyes and didn't look at anything. Sometimes it comforted me to know that I didn't have to look at anything.

And people began to form an image of me as this rather arrogant person because of the way I looked at them. I told myself I should reinvent myself according to this image. I also stubbornly thought that I should become shier and kinder to fight against this image. I ended up being neither.

After school I made friends with animals. I couldn't really see very well in the evening anyway. In the alley behind the school, I had many friends. Girl friends. We held hands. At times we cried and hugged. We then went into our own rooms and wrote letters. About a longing we didn't understand. Love letters.

When I wrote in large handwriting, I felt I was getting closer to the object. It's nice to write something, I thought, and I liked it. To like something. To be able to say I like something without hesitation was most exhilarating.

Words were similar to me, but they weren't me. I felt someone was telling me about one of my selves who'd lived a long time ago, of whom I was ignorant. I also felt I was getting closer to one of your selves, of whom you were ignorant.

To feel the part of the world I didn't know about in close proximity, I have a habit of studying things closely. And since I don't know if what I'm writing is accurate, I write in great detail. I have to concentrate in order to make my writing dense. If I don't, it becomes the wrong shape. When trying to describe a world beyond reality, it's not enough to look at reality. I need details. I need to be sensitive.

I learned that I can give things a three-dimensional feel by describing a small part of a whole in new and fresh ways. And that the small, sensitive part grows stronger over time. The small part that I described eventually became a container for the whole. The small part wove perfectly fitting clothes for the animals. *What can be easily seen might not be all that important*, we said, *arms around one another. Something very small, but very precious, I would like to have something like that. I want to have things like us, that which are thrown away and loved. Things that are small and precious and make everything feel important.* At the time, we didn't know that the important things would pile up and that we would eventually come face to face with this big thing of great importance.

I tried layering one vivid image on top of another. That was the most important thing, still is. This complex of mine, of not being able to see certain things and having to scrutinize other things, is it a blessing? Or a curse?

If I harness the power of medical technology, I can fix my eye. I might, one day. Everybody does it—but it scares me. Perhaps because I was traumatized. If only I could toughen up my guts, if only I could bear the pain of a foreign object entering my eye. If only I had the courage to step out of the beautiful ruin I've lived in ever since it became impossible for me to be equal to something . . .

I'm filled with pain, but every day I dream of overcoming the pain. I want to be happy. Apparently there is an opinion in the medical community to categorize happiness as an illness. I want to have that illness. But happiness lasts only a moment, and

I continue to write. Until when? While writing, I am in exile. Poems render me an exile. Poems become a road for the exile.

The layers of images in text speak to one another and create something new. My eye, like a ray of light, comes alive in a sentence. Sentences are cruel, but they shine. The more I fail, the more they shine.

COMMENTARY

There's a Light
That's Darker Than Darkness

Kim Na-young (Literary Critic)

In "Ars Poetica," Archibald MacLeish writes, "A poem should not mean / But be." The meaning of the lines can be examined through the context of the era that he lived in. When the First World War broke out, as someone who had relinquished the means to a comfortable life and fled to a foreign country, MacLeish began to write about the immense despair that enveloped individual lives and the anxiety of humanity at large. Thus, his poems invariably draw a picture of despair beyond despair, anxiety beyond anxiety. The narratives are familiar to those who lead difficult lives; the reason his poems have prevailed nonetheless must be that there is a role that poems alone can fulfill within such lives, situated at the site where distinguishing between meaning and meaninglessness becomes unnecessary.

This collection of Lee Young-ju's poems can be said to undermine the existence of her other collections-to-date. Most new poetry collections extend the ideas in the preceding collections (regardless of whether the thread has been extended singularly), but this collection does not, and the departure demands scrutiny. The question is no longer how the poems in the new collection say something new, but rather why their existence denies the poetic world that Lee Young-ju has built over a long period of time.

The poems don't argue right and wrong; they

place meaning on their words being "spoken."
Why the poems should be read in such a way can
be explained through a question; as Lee Young-ju
writes in "House of Tears," "Why do we put so much
effort into maintaining our form when we're dead?"
Treating life as though it went on, when in fact it
has stopped—what gives rise to this attitude? Why
do some lives exist to inform other lives that a life
can be maintained in the form of an early death?
This question feels urgent because it presupposes
the loss of a life.

What remains in the wake of a loss. This collection
of Lee Young-ju's poems showcase such a paradoxical
mode of existence. ("This story begins from the
ruins." —from "The Daily Life of a Café Owner"). For
example, to someone who has experienced the loss
of a loved one and of meaning in the world they used
to share with the loved one, their life, which signifies
nothing but the meaninglessness of the world in

which they now belong, is just another name for time. When words and meaning fail. When the only way to go on living is by negating a meaning-filled world. The poems in this collection appear to be born of such a time, depicting a life that has swallowed a death, or some other great loss.

That these poems, sentences, and words—these breaths—can mean something different to each reader is indicative of the fact that they are, above all, meaningless. Meaningless meaning that has been rescued from the fractured lives, honest in its truth, is what the poems in this collection manage to substantiate.

"To flow away" or "to drift away" is a motif that recurs throughout the collection. It exists to prove that there is something that flows. To those who have witnessed the death of a family member, death isn't a singular event that brings a life to an end. Because in those moments after the loved one has died, in those moments when they live as though they were dead, they live through death, not only as they come face to face with deathly moments of their own, but also as they burrow into unbearable memories. Lee Young-ju depicts the flow of this paradoxical system of life. Life is discovered within the flow, and that which is adrift can continue to drift if and only if it also effects the flow.

Such a nightmarish life from which one cannot wake on their own is detailed in "House of Tears" (in remembrance of the Jeju uprising) and "The Neighborhood of Daebang": "In the deepest basement, the bones of the boy flow through the veins of the water"; "My ailment flowed toward a place I was trying to get to, the road beyond the stairs, beyond the evening, where clenched teeth melted away." The sadness beyond sadness, the despair beyond despair questions whether language could exist, what it might mean to speak, in such a world. Because where words cannot reach, lives beyond death are being led, those lives that are more like death than death.

How can there be darkness that makes one feel more helpless than darkness itself? The question is a weighty answer that this collection gives us. If meaning and reason are born in the arrangement of words, there is a life born of the kind of arrangement that renders meaning and reason irrelevant. We look away from such a life, the kind of life that asks what a god is, the kind of life in which one affirms that one is alive by digging under one's fingernails; in other words, we know that there are "children who survive him," but we lead our lives pretending we don't ("Dyer"). If such a life is part of what we mean when we speak of life, how can we remain blind to it? How can we continue to ignore it?

"Since I'm not dead, I can't stop writing," Lee Young-ju says. To live is to write, and death is what brings those two acts together, is what Lee seems to say; her perspective allows her to mourn the deaths of many and the lives of those who are left behind. In Lee's fourth collection Keep No Record of Love (Moonji Publishing), many of the poems speak to the incident involving the Sinking of MV Sewol, but one can also engage in a decontextualized reading; for example, in "Blank Notes," she writes, "A conversation so quiet that it's beyond anyone's understanding unless someone writes it down." In this quiet sentence is a burning will to record those voices of the weak. This will is also the driving force behind many of her poems, derived from her resolve to write down another's voice and the difficulty inherent in the task. "If writing can cause pain, what am I supposed to do in this place full of letters?" she writes ("Egypt Boy" from Keep No Record of Love). If she sounds hesitant, it's because she cherishes her despair as a poet, one who speaks, one who writes, one who must always wonder, "What does it mean for me to write this?"

Lee Young-ju writes as a citizen and a poet, about what has happened and the pain that is ongoing; this peculiar blend of subjects and perspectives have become her means of finding certainty. She isn't satisfied with recording the event and despair as-is; she excavates the brutality that lies within the "as-is," while recognizing that no words can adequately describe what she sees. She argues against all those who say to the mourners, "That's enough." Her poems shine brightly in the imagination of death, as though to prove there's a light that's darker than darkness.

WHAT
THEY SAY
ABOUT
LEE YOUNG-JU

POET

Her poems are her. She encompasses, by way of her feminine embrace, the cruelest social epic (which is the current state of affairs), most sensitive and teeming with life, in order to depict cruelty, the truth behind life and sensation; though she is a bit strange and suspicious, she is serene, composed, and lulling; her suggestions are so natural and organic that she brings pain to a poet's heart. Even that which lies beyond this poet's heart is a part of her and one of her poems.

Kim Jung-whan (Poet)

Poet Lee Young-ju's hand cuts. It excises the very small, very thin layer of parasitic sadness that resides in all living and inanimate beings. A letter, sugar, a story, a mother . . . I imagine she holds them in her white, outstretched palm. First she looks at them, then she begins to dissect them. The scene that unfolds in my mind makes my skin crawl, makes me want to cry. The day I met her—this poet who would spend her life with that hand at the end of her arm—I saw a nascent wind emerge from her fingertips.

Kang Ji-hye (Poet)

K-Poet
You Arrived in the Season of Perennial Summer

Written by Lee Young-ju | **Translated by** Jae Kim
Published by ASIA Publishers | 445, Hoedong-gil, Paju-si, Gyeonggi-do, Korea
(Seoul Office: 161-1, Seodal-ro, Dongjak-gu, Seoul, Korea)
Homepage Address www.bookasia.org | **Tel** (822).821.5055 | **Fax** (822).821.5057
ISBN 979-11-5662-317-5 (set) | 979-11-5662-494-3 (04810)
First published in Korea by ASIA Publishers 2020

This book is published with the support of the Literature Translation Institute of Korea
(LTI Korea).

K-픽션 한국 젊은 소설

최근에 발표된 단편소설 중 가장 우수하고 흥미로운 작품을 엄선하여 출간하는 〈K-픽션〉은 한국문학의 생생한 현장을 국내외 독자들과 실시간으로 공유하고자 기획되었습니다. 원작의 재미와 품격을 최대한 살린 〈K-픽션〉 시리즈는 매 계절마다 새로운 작품을 선보입니다.

Through literature, you
bilingual Edition Modern

ASIA Publishers' carefully selected

Set 1	Set 2

Division
Industrialization
Women

Liberty
Love and Love
Affairs
South and North

Set 3	Set 4

Seoul
Tradition
Avant-Garde

Diaspora
Family
Humor

Search "bilingual edition

can meet the real Korea!
Korean Literature

22 keywords to understand Korean literature

Set 5

Relationships

Discovering

Everyday Life

Taboo and Desire

Set 6

Fate

Aesthetic Priests

The Naked in the

Colony

Set 7

Colonial Intellectuals Turned "Idiots"

Traditional Korea's Lost Faces

Before and After Liberation

Korea After the Korean War

korean literature"on Amazon!